# HANNAH'S JOURNAL

❧ THE STORY OF AN IMMIGRANT GIRL ❧

S

5.2

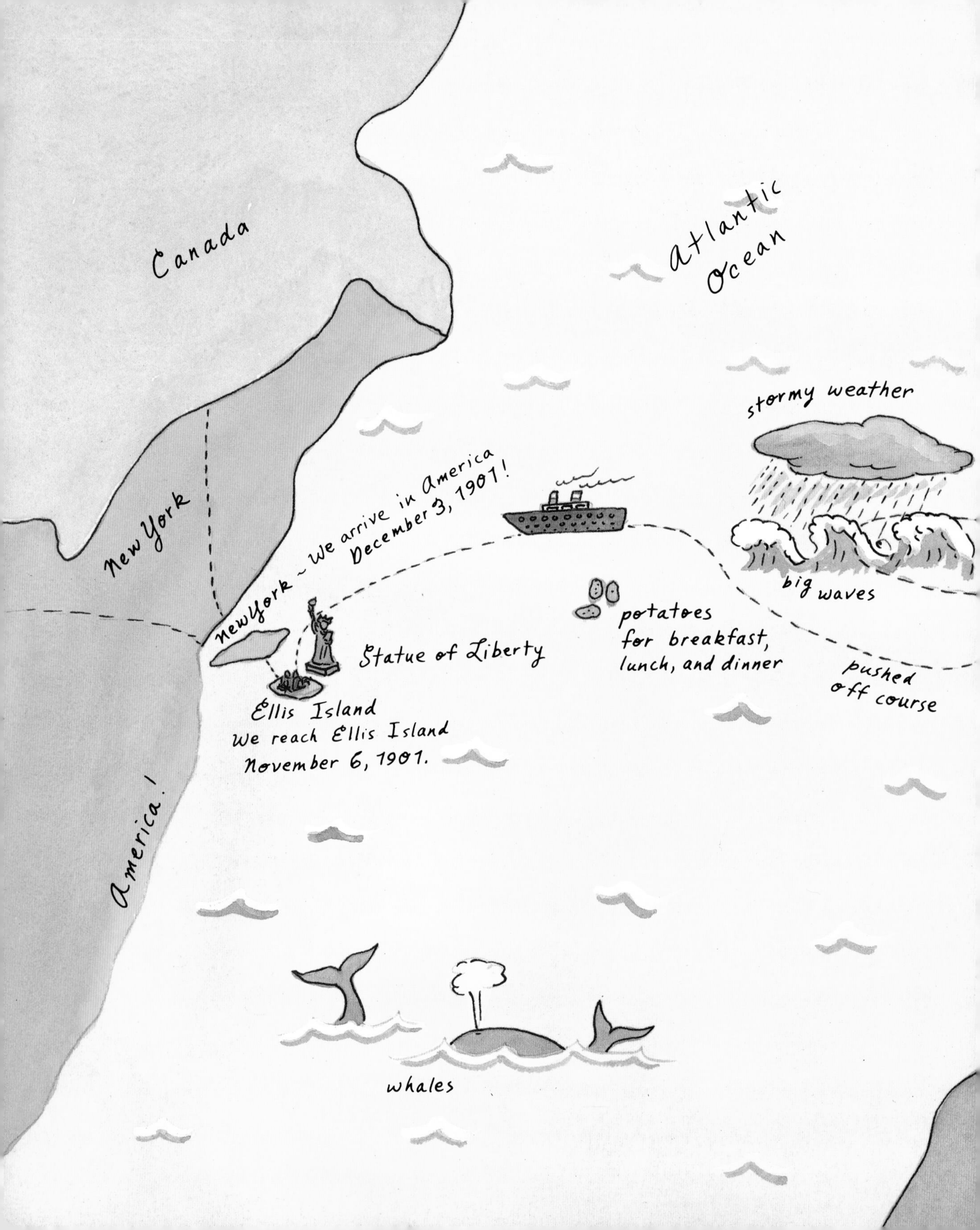

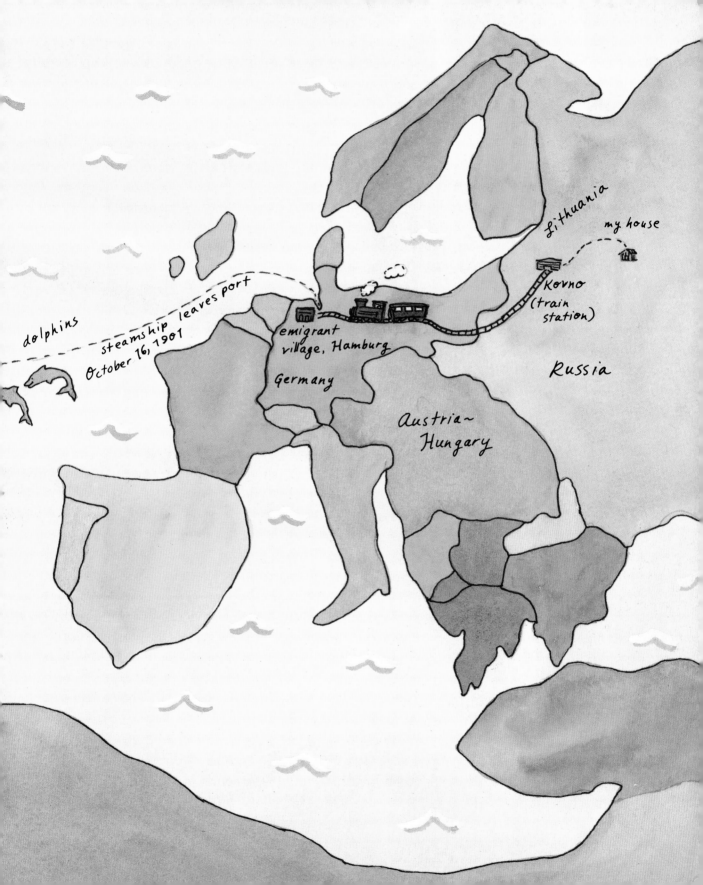

HAMBURG - AMERIKA LINIE        "Atlanta"

# HANNAH'S JOURNAL

## ❧ THE STORY OF AN IMMIGRANT GIRL ❧

*Marissa Moss*

*Silver Whistle*

Harcourt, Inc.

San Diego   New York   London

our hens

To Zwecia Faga Srolowitz
and Samuel Gardner

our house
in Lithuania

Mendel, 3 years old

Avram, 5 years old

Isaac, 7 years old

me, Hannah ~ I am the middle child, the only girl of 7 children!

Hershel, 12 years old

Solomon, 14 years old

Isadore, 16 years old

## September 27, 1901

Today is my birthday. I am now ten years old and Papashka gave me this journal to write in. All this paper just for me! He knows how much I want to learn, so now even though I cannot go to school like my brothers, I can practice sums and copy lessons in here. Hershel said he would teach me Hebrew, and Solomon will help me with Russian. I do not want to have a head as empty as a leaky old kettle.

Here is the start of the Hebrew alphabet. I like how strong the letters look, like living tree branches.

דּ גּ בּ א
dalet gimel bet aleph

Hebrew is like a secret mirror code because you read it backwards.

АБВГДЕЖЗИ

These letters look like they're marching!

Here is the start of the Russian alphabet. Students learn Russian, not Lithuanian, because Lithuania is just a small part of giant Mother Russia.

Mama has a round face, like an apple. She cannot read, but she loves stories.

Here is Papashka. He loves books as much as I do, but he is not a rebbe. He's a clock maker.

While my brothers study, I pluck chickens for the soup pot. Mama says a girl needs clever fingers, not a clever head.

It would be even better to go to school, but heder is only for boys and Papashka cannot pay a tutor for me. "Educating a daughter, that's throwing money out the window," he says. Then he kisses me on the top of my head and whispers, "But for you, I would do it — if I _had_ such money." He would, too, I know it, even if Mama would frown and knit her brow at such a waste.

This was my birthday present from Isadore ~ a postcard of a heder scene. He said it's so I can feel part of a school just by looking at it. Solomon laughed and said all the boys look so frozen in the picture, it would make me relieved _not_ to have to go. They _do_ look cold, but seeing all those books before them makes me hunger to turn the pages with them.

Dancing with Mendel, who is very light on his feet

This journal alone, with its thick creamy paper ~
I shudder to think what it cost. I cried when Papashka
gave it to me ~ so perfect it is!

"Sha, sha, sheyna," he said. "Tears on your birthday?
Smiles, we must have smiles!" And he picked up his fiddle
and started to play. Who could cry then? We all started
dancing ~ the tune would not let our feet stay still. It was
the best of birthdays.

September 30, 1901

Mama sent me to market to get fish for soup tonight.
I love to see all the goods displayed, but even better is to
hear what news is stirring. The men gather around to talk,
and no one notices a small girl in their shadows.

bagel

mama always gives me an extra coin to buy a bagel from old Mirka

Reb Chaim had just received a
letter from his son Zalman in America.
Zalman sent money and wrote that in
America Jews can own land and run
their businesses without worry. No
one bothers them for being Jewish.

letter and stamp all the way from America

Reb Moishe didn't believe it, but others were saying that they, too, wanted to go to America ~ or at least send their own sons to see if it's all true. I try to imagine America, but I can't. The word has a good solid sound to it, though ~ _America_ ~ it _sounds_ like a wonderful place.

October 5, 1901

Uncle Saul and Aunt Chaya came for dinner with Esther, their younger daughter. It was the first time they've visited since Rivka, their older daughter, died of influenza. It felt odd to have just the three of them, as if the family had shrunk into itself, from a plump happy grape to a withered sad raisin. But the sad raisin had an important proposition. And it had to do with _me_!

It seems that before Rivka died six months ago, she was betrothed to Reb Chaim's son ~ Zalman, the one in America. Zalman sent money and a steamship ticket for Rivka to come join him, and Uncle Saul arranged for a passport, travel papers, and the train ticket to the port.

I've always thought Esther would be pretty if she didn't look so glum all the time. Since Rivka's death, she's even more miserable and barely speaks a word. I used to think we'd be good friends (she is, after all, only four years older), but she doesn't even notice me.

# Hamburg-Amerika Linie, Hamburg.

Steamship tickets to America cost $25 ~ that's a fortune and not to be wasted!

But Rivka was afraid to go such a long way by herself, so it was decided that Esther would go, too. (Zalman sent _her_ a steamship ticket, ~~too~~ ~ so much money to be made in America, who could believe it?) Then dear Rivka died. In the midst of mourning, now we had to decide what to do with those tickets.

    Uncle Saul wanted Esther to still go to America. She's only fourteen now, but in a few years, _she_ could wed Zalman.

Rivka's passport

Uncle Saul is Papashka's older brother. He has a small store, so a visit from him always means a special treat. This time he brought us ribbon candy.

Meanwhile, she could earn money and send for her parents and the family would be reunited.

A good plan, we all thought, but what of the other ticket? Isadore and Solomon both wanted it, I could see. Who wouldn't want a chance to go to this golden country, this America?

Isadore's ears turn bright red when he's excited.

If I had that ticket, I could earn the money quickly to send for the family.

Perhaps so, however the papers are in Rivka's name, and you don't look like a Rivka.

"Nu," continued Uncle Saul. "My brother ~ your father, that is ~ and I have talked it over, and we've decided it's Hannah who should go."

Me! I couldn't believe it. Me! I have never been out of our shtetl. To go all the way to America? Was it possible?

Isadore was not about to give up so easily. "But she is no more a Rivka than I am! Does Hannahle look sixteen?"

Now it was Esther's turn to blush, she who is already as round as Rivka was, while I am still a stick. I hadn't dared dream of America before, but once the ticket was offered to me, I wanted it more than anything.

"Esther looks sixteen," I said. "She can use Rivka's papers and I can use hers. If I part my hair to the side,

Which was sweeter? The candy or the gift of the golden ticket? I savored both.

"Hmmm," said Uncle Saul. "Hmmm," said Papashka. I could see they thought Isadore was right. I had to say something.

there's a likeness. I may not look sixteen, but fourteen, that's possible."

Papashka stroked his beard and nodded. "See, she has a good head on her shoulders. Such a one could make the journey. She will be the one to send us all tickets."

Mama shook her head. "Such nonsense. She's a mere slip of a girl."

"Mama," I begged, "give me a chance. In America maybe I can go to school. I'll finally have a chance to fill my head!"

Papashka roared with laughter. "Such a child! Everyone else wants the gold ~ she wants the knowledge. Doesn't she deserve to go?"

"I'll think about it," Mama said, and that was the last word. (Mama always has the last word.) I'll just have to show her that I can help my family, even if I am a slip of a girl.

October 8, 1901

Before yesterday Mama didn't want me to go to America. After yesterday, she, too, wants me to go ~ as quickly as possible. In America there are no pogroms.

It began just as we sat down to dinner. From far off

came sounds of guns shooting. Then the shots came nearer and we could hear glass breaking and women shrieking.

At the first gunshot, Mama's face went white. Papashka quickly herded us all out of the house. We ran after him, Mama carrying Mendel, me pulling Avram and Isaac by their hands. We rushed to the Lybovs' house. He's the tax assessor, and Papashka says he's honest and doesn't hate the Jews.

Papashka pounded on the door as we all huddled around him. Down the street, I saw angry men throwing rocks through windows, tearing doors open and flinging beds, pots, books into the mud. I saw one man beat Reb Chaim with a stick. Another shot Reb Shlomo's cow right in the head. I was scared, so scared. I have never before been so scared. It was worse than any nightmare I've ever had, only I was awake.

Avram and Isaac didn't cry. We were all quiet. Only Papashka made noise, pounding on the door. What if it

Later I asked Papashka who the men were and why they did this. He said they were peasants who blamed the Jews for their troubles. When things went badly for them, they came to punish us. I don't understand why it's _our_ fault.

Mr. Lybov

He need not fear the peasants ~ a tax assessor is an important person, so Papashka said we were not endangering Mr. Lybov by going to _his_ house.

broken chairs, tables, doors, feather pillows, crockery, glass

never opened? What would become of us?

Then it opened, the door opened, like a blessing falling upon us. The tax assessor stood there. For a moment I feared he would shut the door again, he looked so surprised to see us. Then another shot fired and, without a word, he quickly pulled us all inside. Papashka was trembling. We were all trembling. But now, safe inside the house, Mendel, Isaac, and Avram all erupted in noisy sobs.

Mrs. Lybov brought us tea and egg cookies. She said everything would be all right. "It happens now and then," she said, "but it will all be over soon, you'll see. You'll clean up and all will be just as before."

I thought nothing would ever be the same for me, nothing would be all right. How could I ever feel safe again? In silence we sipped our tea with lips stiff from fear and listened to the sounds of glass and wood breaking outside.

At last it was quiet. The pogrom was over. Old Mirka, the bagel woman, was killed, and Reb Chaim was badly beaten, but Mama said our shtetl was lucky. In some pogroms many people die. We should be

I know she was old, but I will still miss her.

It was so strange ~ drinking tea from these elegant glasses while outside, all was dark and ugly.

The full moon was high in the sky when we finally left the tax assessor's house. Everything was wrapped in a thick hush. The moonlight shone on streets strewn with glass and splintered wood.

grateful for only one death. A bitter thanks, if you ask me. Mama said we were lucky, but when we came to our house, I saw the tears stream down her cheeks. Our beds were torn to tatters and the straw stuffing strewn everywhere. Every plate was broken. Every window was smashed. Flour dusted the floors, someone's boot had crushed Papashka's fiddle, and his silver kiddush cup, our one piece of silver, handed down from his father's father to his father and then to him, was gone, stolen.

Papashka covered his face ~ he could bear to see no more.

I don't know what he grieved over more ~ the loss of the cup or the fiddle. Either way, his heart was broken.

How will Shabbat be the same without Papashka's cup for the blessing over the wine? <u>Nothing can be the same now.</u>

We swept and cleaned and saved what we could. After we had made up new beds and put the little ones to sleep, Mama turned to me and said, "Hannah, listen to me. This should never happen to us again. NEVER! You must go to America and work as hard as you can. We will be waiting, waiting to come join you." She looked around at our broken home, then back at me.

"It won't be long, Mama," I promised. And I mean it. I had thought going to America would be a grand adventure,

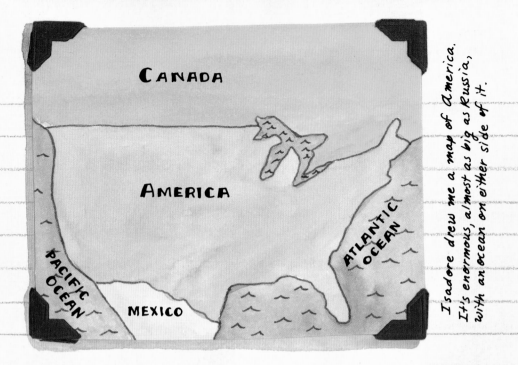

but now I know it is more than that. It is hope for all my family. It is our chance to live free of this horrible fear. It is a chance to mend Papashka's heart. And maybe, maybe it will be my chance to learn.

October 10, 1901

These past days have been bittersweet, knowing they are the last with my family until

These last days in our shtetl are like the sandwich we make during the Passover seder, both bitter with bitter herbs and sweet with honeyed haroset. I taste the two together ~ I want to go and I want to stay.

who knows when. How I will miss them all! Especially my Papashka. I always feel so treasured by him, like he sees straight into my heart. I'll be so alone without him.

Isadore insists that he will earn his own passage to America and then the two of us can work twice as quickly to bring the rest. By next Passover we'll all be together again, he says.

embroidered tablecloth

pewter candlesticks

Mama made the tablecloth herself. She was saving it for my dowry ~ now, she says, I must take my dowry with me. We have so little left after the pogrom, I didn't want to take anything, but Mama insisted.
"I'll feel better knowing you have a bit of our home with you," she said.

From his lips to God's ear!
October 11, 1901

Tonight is my last night with my family. In the morning I start the long journey to America. Mama has packed a satchel for me with a Shabbat tablecloth, a pair of candlesticks, a chang of clothes, a loaf of bread, dried fruit, and a photograph, so when I get sad or lonely, I can be with my family again.

Papashka gave me a prayer book. "You can pray," he said, "and practice Hebrew at the same time. You can start studying to be an American now." But in America, I wonder, do they

The prayer book was Papashka's father's. I know how much it means to him, especially with the kiddush cup gone, and yet he gave it to me. Inside the front cover my grandfather's name is written in spidery script. Underneath is Papashka's name, and under that, Papashka added _my_ name.

speak Hebrew? Yiddish? Will anyone understand me? And how will _I_ understand anyone? Oh, Papashka, I want to go, but it's so hard to leave.

October 12, 1901

I must have kissed Papashka's beard a thousand times. I hugged Mama so tight my arms ached. But my heart ached more. Still, I had to go. Uncle Saul drove Esther and me in his cart to the train station. I turned back and watched my house, my family, my world disappear from sight ~ and like Lot's wife, I felt like a frozen block of bitter salt, like dried-up tears.

Then we reached the station. So many people, more people than I'd ever seen, made me remember where I'm going and how important it is to all my family that I succeed.

With a clatter and a roar, puffs of steam hissing from the sides, the great black bulk of the train pulled into the station. I felt like I was about to step into some strange machine that would hurl me into the future.

If Papashka had been there, leaving would have been impossible,

Esther's eyes were big and black with fear. If she could have sunk into the earth, she would have.

Poor Uncle Saul. I hadn't thought of how he must feel leaving Esther ~ now he has _no_ children at home.

but with only Uncle Saul to say good-bye to, it wasn't as hard. But poor Esther. Uncle had to take her by the shoulders and put her on the train. The huge crowd on the platform surged forward. Everyone was shoving and I felt caught up in the anxious wave of people. If we didn't hurry, we wouldn't get a place. Still, Esther dragged herself so slowly, I was tempted to push her through.

As it was, all the seats by the windows were taken. I so wanted to see all the countryside pass by, but we were wedged tightly between two fat grandmothers ~ one smelled like garlic, the other reeked of sausage. Surrounded by the tightly packed crowd, we were all alone for the first time in our lives.

The train had long, narrow benches and raised-up places where people put their baskets and trunks, clutching smaller parcels on their laps. It smelled like herring and onion and unwashed hair and stale breath and tobacco and too many bodies all scrunched together. Oh, for a window and some fresh air!

When we stop at stations, peddlers offer all kinds of wares through the windows.

Passengers lean out with coins and barter for the goods.

October 13, 1901

I like the rythm of the train, the song the wheels make in my head, but my stomach lurches whenever we stop. Then when the engine starts again and picks up speed, I feel dizzy with how fast the world rushes by in the windows (a good thing, after all, that I'm not closer to them).

Esther has said scarcely a word this whole time (while the grandmother next to me wears my ear down with countless stories of her no-good daughter-in-law. Sometimes I pretend to sleep just to stop her constant whining.) I thought this train trip would give me a chance to get to know Esther, but when I talk to her she gives one-word answers and closes her eyes. (Pretending to sleep to shut me out!) What is going on in her head? Last night I heard her crying ~quietly, so as not to disturb anyone. Instead of having a friend on this journey, I have a timid mouse I must constantly take care of.

October 14, 1901

We've arrived in Hamburg, where the steamship waits. I have never seen such a beautiful and big city! When the train pulled into the station (a grand brick building, not a small wooden one like the others), I leaped up with my satchel, so eager was I to get off that train and out into the colors, light, and air of the city. Esther just sat there,

The train trip was over, but the real journey was about to begin. Could we really cross an ocean? I've never seen one, but I imagine it as huge.

like oil on a puddle. "Esther, we're here," I said. "Let's go!"

"Go?" she echoed hollowly. "Go where? What are we to do now? Where are we to go? How are we to find the harbor? The steamship? And then all the way to America? No, it's not possible."

That was more than I'd heard her say the whole trip.

"What do you mean, 'not possible'?" I thought of the promise I'd made to Mama. "We have tickets. We're going." I pulled on her sleeve, but I couldn't pull her up. She was the older one, but I could see there was no relying on her. I would have to get us to the steamship ~ I would have to take care of everything. The problem was, I didn't know where to go any more than she did. But at least I was determined to find out.

The train had emptied out around us. "Come, follow me," I said. "I'll find the way."

And for the first time, she looked at me. "You will?"

The station was full of people — soldiers with guns (we stayed far away from them), wealthy women in furs and gloves, men hurrying busily, peddlers selling food ~ but no one I dared ask for help.

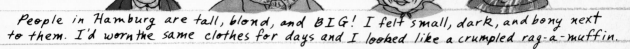

People in Hamburg are tall, blond, and BIG! I felt small, dark, and bony next to them. I'd worn the same clothes for days and I looked like a crumpled rag-a-muffin.

I nodded and I must have looked sure of myself, because after that she followed me meekly like a lamb. As long as I told her what to do, she was all right. It was strange, but being in charge of her made me less worried about myself.

I led Esther out of the station, but on the street, it was no clearer which was the right direction. The buildings were so tall, I couldn't see where the harbor was.

We just stood there for a while, Esther patiently waiting for me to choose a path. We would probably be there still, but for a boy who walked up to us. He was eight, maybe ten years old, his clothes and face grimy with dirt, but there was a sparkle in his eye and he held himself with pride.

"Ladies," he said, and he meant us, Esther
The boy looked like my cousin Yakov.

and me ~ ladies, indeed! "I offer you my services as a guide. Pay me in bread and cheese, and I'll take you where you want to go." He looked at my satchel and Esther's trunk. "You're leaving on the steamship <u>Atlanta</u> for America, no? I can take you to the steamship offices. You must present all your papers there first before you can board."

My satchel wasn't very heavy, but Esther's trunk felt like it was loaded with cobblestones.

"How do you know so much?" I asked. "How do you know we're going to America? Is it written on our foreheads?"

The boy smiled. "I'm right, aren't I? Of course I am."

He was infuriating! I scowled at him. "We don't need your help."

"Ah, I think you do," he insisted. "My name is Samuel and I'm taking the <u>Atlanta</u> to America, too." He picked up Esther's trunk and hoisted it easily to his scrawny shoulder. "Come, I'll show you the way. If you like, we can travel together."

I grabbed for the trunk. "How do I know you're not a thief?" I could see Esther was frozen with fear. She would be no help.

Samuel set down the trunk with a thud. "Fine, lug it yourself." But I still didn't know <u>where</u> I should lug it.

There we stood, facing each other like two roosters. Finally I blurted out, "But you're just a boy! How can you know where to go and what to do?"

He smiled that grin again. "A boy can be clever, can't he? I've come all the way from Minsk, in Russia. I can make it to America, easy as pie."

The buildings in Hamburg are tall and close together. Will America be like this?

I chewed my lip. What choice did I have? I would have to trust him and hope he was telling the truth. He was certainly dirty enough to have come all the way from Minsk.

"Then show us the way," I said. "And you can carry the trunk."

Esther gaped at me like a fish, but I just grabbed her hand tight and pulled her along.

October 15, 1901

I was too tired to write more last night, but now I've had a good night's sleep ~ in a bed, no less. Samuel brought us to an emigrant village built especially for people to stay in while they wait for their ship to embark. A whole village just for people, like us, going to America! Samuel did know where to go after all.

The village is bigger than our shtetl! It even has a synagogue and a kosher kitchen.

Today we are to meet him in front of the offices, and together we'll show our papers. Then we can board the steamship. Sometime today we'll be on our way to America! Esther isn't excited like me. She's terrified of what lies ahead. I don't know what scares her more ~ the sea voyage or landing in a strange new country.

I'm traveling with a baby, it seems. But at least I don't have to change her diapers!

October 16, 1901

So much to write, I don't know where to begin! When we got to the steamship office, Esther had a sudden fit of panic. What if they saw that we were using someone else's

*Once again I had to push Esther through a door. Will I spend this whole trip pushing and pulling a balking mule?*

papers? Would we be clapped in jail? Or would our money be taken from us, leaving us stranded in Hamburg? Every awful thing that could happen, she imagined. Samuel made things worse, yelling at Esther that she was a stupid mule and deserved a good hard kick. "Doesn't she realize how lucky she is to go?" he shouted. I glared at him and put my arm around her, trying to think what Mama and Papashka would say.

"Sha, sha, sheyna," I soothed. "Everything's fine. You'll pass for Rivka. I _know_ it." But she just kept sobbing and begging to go home. Finally I took her by the shoulders and shook her _hard_. "Listen, Esther, we _must_ go. Think of our families. We can't leave them there ~ don't you remember the pogrom? In America we'll have no troubles."

"Troubles!" she snapped. She looked just like a turtle, her mouth pursed into a sharp beak. "_You'll_ have no troubles. _You_ don't have to marry a stranger in a strange land, with no mother or father to bless you."

*Mendel likes to play with the snapping turtles in the pond behind our house, but they frighten me, and Esther scares me, too, sometimes. She can be so quiet, then suddenly she erupts.*

The steamship was immense, like the big fish that swallowed Jonah. I felt dizzy walking up the ramp, being swallowed by that monster.

"Is _that_ it?" I was angry, but I tried to speak calmly. "Nu, what's the problem? You can wait until your parents join you in America to get married. But first _you_ have to get there to earn their tickets, no? _That's_ what's most important."

After all that fuss, no one even studied our papers. The agent glanced at them, but he looked more carefully at us. If we weren't healthy, we wouldn't be allowed on board. Fortunately Esther's nervousness wasn't considered a disease, and Samuel, freshly washed, even looked handsome. And me, I must have passed the agent's examination, because before I could worry about failing, we were on our way into the biggest ship I'd seen, a ship big enough to hold dozens of trains and so many people, they were beyond counting. Entering the ship was already like going to another country ~ what would America be like?

Such scenes by that ship! People crying as if their hearts would break as they said good-bye ~ parent to child, husband to wife. How I missed my dear ones then!

ceiling

Samuel took the top bunk.

I took the middle.

Esther curled up miserably on the bottom bunk, and we stored our things below it.

floor

The beds are wooden bunks, one on top of the other. Samuel suggested we all take top bunks because the air is fresher, but we decided to take one whole row so we would only clamber on top of each other.

How to describe it? Our quarters are in a place called <u>steerage</u>. I think it should be called <u>storage</u> because we are packed together like potatoes in a bin. We're on the lowest level of the ship, on the same deck as all the machinery ~ the din from the engines is constant. The engine noise is matched, however, by the many, many voices of people. So many people in so many different languages! I hear German, Russian, Yiddish, Hungarian, Polish, Lithuanian, Romanian, Croatian ~ I don't even know all the names of the languages I hear.

I think the family next to us are gypsies ~ their clothes look ragged but are brightly colored. The mother and the grandmother have big gold hoops in their ears and many jingling necklaces of gold coins. They look poor, but they have food, and better still, they have each other. How I wish I could make this journey with my family!

The first thing the grandmother did was start a small fire and peel some potatoes for soup. I was afraid she would set the ship on fire! I'm sure it's not allowed, but no one has stopped her so far.

The grandfather smokes his pipe and uses a trunk for a seat. (You can't sit up in the bunks, only lie down.)

The mother filled a tub with water and set about bathing the baby.

The whole family seems so prepared and comfortable.

My stomach rumbled when I smelled the soup. On Samuel's advice we had boiled a dozen eggs and bought more bread and cheese to eat on board ship. Meals are served, but Esther worries they won't be kosher, so it's best for us to feed ourselves.

Soon enough, though, the stink of smoke, of piss, of unwashed bodies mixed with the smell of garlic, onion, and potatoes, and whatever appetite I had was completely lost.

October 18, 1901

The smells are the worst part of this trip! Even worse than the noise! I've discovered that the best way to keep from getting seasick is to spend as much time on the deck as possible. Down in steerage the air is so thick with the smell of other people's vomit, it's enough to make my stomach heave even without the pitch and roll of the ship.

I love to stare at the ocean. I've never seen so much water before ~ all the way to the horizon. It's like staring into a starry night sky, and seeing all that empty space makes me feel less crowded even though I'm surrounded by people.

Samuel scampers around the ship, running errands for the passengers in first class. He's paid in candy, apples, or oranges. My favorites are the oranges he shares with me ~ such a strange fruit. The first time, I tried to just bite into one, but the outside was rubbery and hard to sink my teeth into. I thought he was playing a trick on me! Samuel laughed and showed me how to tear the peel away. Underneath is a ball you can pull apart into separate pieces that are easy to eat. It's a juicy fruit, mostly water, not at all like an apple. After the dirty water we have to drink, an orange is a real treat.

*orange, with peel on*

*the inside part you eat*

The first-class passengers all look like kings and queens, even finer than the people in the Hamburg train station. But their most precious jewel, I think, is English. I try to catch what words I can. Even though I don't know what they mean, I repeat them to myself over and over, savoring how they sound and how they feel in my mouth.

Oddly enough, one woman, who is clearly very wealthy, walks a dog that's more of an overgrown rat.

Another reason to avoid steerage is all the lice. They spread so easily from head to head. Mama's always been so careful to keep our hair clean. When I see someone scratching their head, I get as far away as I can.

If I could, I'd sleep on deck, but the ship's crew won't let us. They curse at us and call us human filth~ to them we're cargo. But we wouldn't be so dirty if there were a place to wash. The sinks in the washroom were used to clean clothes and dishes as well as people, and they're all clogged up now.

Even worse are the toilets! They're dark, filthy, and reeking. I can't even poke my head in without wanting to retch. The first day, it's true, they were clean, but even then I was afraid to use them. What if a fish  swam up the hole and bit my bottom? I do what everyone else does ~ perch over the rail and use my skirts so no one can see what shouldn't be seen.

October 23, 1901

Poor Esther is still ill. This journey is complete misery to her, but I'm excited by all the new things I'm discovering. The world is so much bigger than ever I imagined!

Samuel, pissing through the rails. He says the tricky part is to test which direction the wind is blowing first and then select the side of the ship accordingly. Otherwise, the wind whips the piss right back on you!

The fish looked like this, and there were at least a dozen of them.

They had smiling mouths and eyes.

Today Samuel and I were standing at the front of the boat (it's called the _prow_), and suddenly we saw these big fishes leaping out of the sea alongside us. Someone said they're called _dolphins_ and should bring us good luck. I hope so. I feel lucky just seeing them ~ they are so beautiful to watch!

October 28, 1901

The last few days have been a nightmare! There was a terrible storm with huge waves like gray iron walls slapping into the ship. We had to stay belowdecks, and the ship was pitching about so much that everything that wasn't tied down went flying across the room. Kettles, pails of vomit, trunks, satchels, and blankets ~ all slid or heaved back and forth.

It felt like the boat was made of twigs and leaves, like the toy ones Isaac had made at home.

angry tall waves ~ was this the luck the dolphins brought?

It was too dark to read and I read Hebrew haltingly anyway, but holding Papashka's prayer book was as good as praying.

Samuel tied Esther's trunk to the post of our bunks and I held my satchel tight. We all crowded onto the upper bunk, as it was least likely to be hit by flying objects. I tried not to be sick, but we all were. It seemed like everyone in that dank, dark, fetid hole was moaning and crying.

I couldn't see Samuel's face, but I know Esther and I were green.

In the middle of all the blackness, Samuel started telling us the story of his family. His voice was calm and steady, like a warm blanket on my wretchedness; and even though what he told was horrible, his telling it to us was a great comfort, I can't say why. It made me feel like he is truly a brother to me.

This is his story. I wrote it down, just like he said it.

## Samuel's Story

My father was very wealthy. I know I don't look rich, but believe me, we were. We lived in Russia, outside of Minsk, on a vast estate. Because my father had supplied the tsar with rifles,

Samuel's favorite horse was a roan named Mincha.

 He loved to feed her apples.

he was given a special land grant. (As a Jew, of course he couldn't actually own the land, but the grant was as close as he could get to that.) There were nine of us children, and we all had private tutors who came to our house to teach us. We had good things to eat, books to read, stoves to warm ourselves, and horses to ride. What more could we want? Nothing! It was a blessed life. But the Cossacks hated my father and said he had no right to the land. One day they came. My mother hid us children under a secret trapdoor and gave us her jewelry so if anything should happen to her, at least we would have that. The nine of us sat huddled in the dark. We could hear big boots stamping overhead, doors slamming, heavy furniture being pushed around. Once some footsteps came very near the trapdoor.

We scarcely dared to breathe, so frightened were we of being found.

Cossack boots

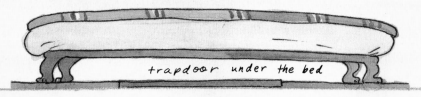
trapdoor under the bed

Then it was quiet. For a long time it was quiet. Finally Misha, my oldest brother, dared to poke his head out. All was dark silence. He pulled himself up through the door and we waited to hear what he saw. It seemed an eternity before he came back. "Are they gone? Is it safe to come out?" we asked. His face was pale and he didn't answer. I knew then that something was dreadfully wrong. He just stood there, then he slumped to the floor and started crying.

The Cossacks, you see, had killed my mother and father. They killed our tutors, and even the servants didn't escape unharmed. Only Grisha, the idiot stable boy, was left alive, babbling about the blood, the blood, oh so much blood.

We left our house that day. Misha divided up the jewels so we would each have money, and because we couldn't agree what to do next, we split up. Misha and Pesya, the two oldest, took the four youngest and headed for Palestine. Malka and Leo, the next oldest, went to South America, to Argentina, because we have an uncle living there. But me, I wanted to go to America. Because in America, I'd heard, a Jew can truly be free.

pouch of jewels

This is how I imagined Samuel's house to look as he told us his story.

As suddenly as it had begun, the storm stopped, and with it, the pitching and rolling. Samuel and I both raced eagerly upstairs, gulping the fresh air greedily. We left poor Esther to clean things up, but I didn't care. I just _had_ to get into the wind and light.

above, big pillowy clouds smiled at us as if the storm had been a mere tantrum.

Breathing the crisp air together, I thought of Samuel in that dark hiding place, like the belly of the ship, coming up to find not relief but horror. I turned to him and touched his arm lightly. "I'm sorry about your family." His story chilled me to the bones. It reminded me of all my fears for _my_ family.

Samuel pulled a gold locket from his pocket. "Would you like to see my mother? This is all I have left of hers."

I nodded. He opened up the locket. Inside were two compartments ~ one with a lock of red hair, the other with a photograph of a beautiful woman.

"You have her eyes," I said softly.

"I do?" Samuel seemed pleased.

"She would be very proud of you, coming so far by yourself," I added. I thought of Mama and Papashka. I would make _them_ proud and bring them safely to America.

I took Samuel's hand and held it. He had done so much for me ~ taken charge, really, showing Esther and me what to do. It was easy to forget he was just a boy, younger than me, even.

It felt good to hold his hand, to feel I could take care of him.

"Samuel," I said, "since no one is meeting you in America, will you stay with us?"

He smiled. "Yes, I would like that."

I'll sleep better tonight knowing that after we get to America, we'll still be together.

Esther is my cousin and Samuel a complete stranger, but he feels so much more a part of my family. She is a weight on my back, but he is a true friend.

## October 31, 1901

We should have reached America days ago, but the storm pushed us off course. Now we're told it will be another week until we arrive. Another week! Sometimes I think Esther is right and we should have never left!

## November 1, 1901

The delay means we've run out of food and must eat what the ship supplies us with. The only thing we can trust to be kosher is the potatoes, so that's all we eat, for every meal.

A man was buried at sea today. He was old and died sometime in his sleep last night. I think he was Russian. His family wailed so loudly, all the babies on board started to cry, too.

I dream about our quiet little shtetl, but then I hear the glass breaking and the gunshots of the pogrom and I remind myself that nothing here is so bad. Anyway, we won't be on this ship forever. Each day brings us closer to America.

To bury someone at sea, they wrap the body in an old blanket and just toss it overboard.

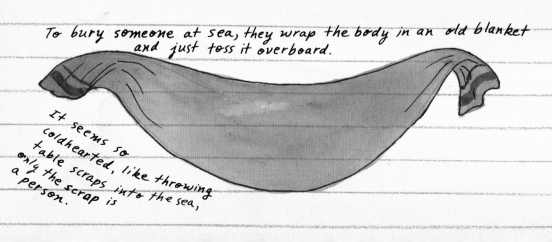

It seems so coldhearted, like throwing table scraps into the sea, only the scrap is a person.

I took out my prayer book and said a prayer of thanks. The men tossed their hats. It was a celebration of sorts.

November 6, 1901

A most magnificent day! We're here at last, in America! Our first sight was of the statue everyone talks about ~ a giant green goddess raising high the torch of Liberty, promising freedom to all who reach her shores. And her other arm holds a book ~ is it a sign I will get the education I've dreamed of?

Everyone crowded on deck to see her. Men cheered. Women waved their kerchiefs. Children clapped excitedly. Even Esther, for the first time since the storm, came out to see the famous statue. She looked so thin and pale in the buttery autumn light, I felt terrible for her. I'd said I'd take care of her, but really I hadn't. I'd avoided steerage as best I could, leaving her to her misery. I promised myself that in America, I'd do better. I'd make sure she was happy and well.

I drew this very, very, very carefully ~ my first sight of America!

ferry boat

As we stood at the rails, a ferry approached our ship. I wished I knew English and could understand what was going on. All I could tell was that men boarded the steamship, names were called, people rushed around, and when the hubbub was over, all the first- and second-class passengers were gone, ferried over to America. Samuel said we must wait for our own ferry, but we wouldn't be taken to America, not yet. First we had to go to an immigration station on Ellis Island.

Ellis Island? I'd never heard of it, but Samuel said it's called the Island of Tears because so many people fail the inspection and get sent back.

Ellis Island is part of America, but we won't officially have entered the country until we cross the harbor into New York. Then we'll truly be in America.

Another inspection? After coming so far, we could be sent back?! I had no idea that was possible! Esther heard the word inspection, and all her fears flooded back. I told her not to worry, I would take care of everything. But in my heart I wondered, what will we do? How can I be sure they let us in?

They pinned tags on us, with our names, the name of the ship, and the number that matches the page on the ship's manifest.

**INSPECTION CARD**
(Immigrants and Steerage Passengers.)

Port of Departure *Hamburg*

Name of Ship *Atlanta*

Name of Immigrant *Rivka Srolowitz*

Last Residence *Lithuania*

Inspected and passed

Passed at quarantine, prt of

Ship's list or manifest

1 2 3 4 5 6 7 8 9 10 11 12 13 14 15 16 17 18 19

We had to answer questions even to get off the ship. The inspector asked me if I could read and write. I was terrified! Would I have to show him this journal? Then I thought of Papashka's prayer book, and I showed how I could read the first page. See, Papashka, it wasn't a waste to teach me. In America, it matters what you know!

Walking a plank from the large steamship to the small ferry made me nervous, but Samuel joked and tried to turn the crossing into a game. He even got a smile out of Esther, tired and fretful though she was.

The ship had been crowded, but that was nothing compared to the numbers on Ellis Island. And now I hear even <u>more</u> languages ~ Greek, Irish, Italian, Turkish, too many to guess at. Long lines snaked everywhere we looked. We stood and stood, and barely moved forward. We weren't even in the building yet!

So many different kinds of clothes! So many different kinds of people!

The gypsy family was in front of us, and just as they had in steerage, they sat on their trunks and set out a picnic. The grandfather took out a fiddle and started to play. I watched them enviously. I wish I had _my_ family with me. I wish _I_ could be so easily comfortable instead of worrying about the coming inspection. Even holding Papashka's prayer book could not soothe my fears. But hearing the fiddle reminded me of my promise to mend Papashka's broken heart. I _would_ bring him to America. I _would_ get him a new fiddle ~ if only I am allowed into America myself!

November 8, 1901

What a terrible

Our things were tagged and stored, until we would be ready to go, but I kept the prayer book with me, our family photograph tucked inside.

day yesterday was! We finally entered the Great Hall ~ it was as big as the Hamburg train station! There were rows and rows of benches, and we sat waiting our turn. But when it came, it was a nightmare ~ they separated us from Samuel! Women went up one staircase, men another. I hugged

While we waited a woman passed out doughnuts and coffee served in cups made out of paper. (You don't keep it. You throw the cup away when you're done ~ imagine that!) My first taste of America, and it was heavenly! The coffee was deliciously hot and sweet. The doughnut looked like a thick, soft bagel, but it tasted light and fluffy and sugary.

Samuel hard and didn't want to let go, but the official barked his harsh English words at me and I had no choice. Samuel promised he would see us again, and then he was gone, his small pointy face swallowed up in a sea of strange men. What if they send him back? What if they send Esther and me back?

Then I was alone with Esther. Why couldn't _she_ have gone and Samuel stayed? Having her was no consolation. I would just have to push her through yet another door.

And it just got worse. Doctors poked at us. We had to undress. (I thought Esther would die of shame, but I had used up all my patience and I yanked off her clothes myself. I wanted to get it all over with, to find Samuel as soon as possible.)

The doctor looked in our eyes, pulling at the lids with a sharp metal hook, inspected our scalps, and put a cold metal disc on our chests. Some women got letters chalked on their coats, an _H_ or _K_ or _Pg_ or _X_. They got taken away. I think those letters are bad marks.

We had to pass a strange test. Some of the questions were like a game.

which face is smiling?

which pictures are identical?

Bad as that was, the next part was even worse. An inspector questioned us one by one. How would I understand him? How would I know what the right answers were? I needed Samuel! And what if the things I said and the things Esther said didn't match? What if they questioned my passport as really being mine? So many what-ifs!

When my turn came, I was so nervous, I could barely speak. At least there was a person who understood Yiddish and translated for me.

The desk was so tall I almost couldn't see the inspector, but what I could see of his face looked stern. Some of the questions were easy ~ like where did I come from and where was I going. Some were hard ~ like was I an anarchist. I don't even know what that means, so I said no.

The only English I could remember from the ship was "please," "thank you," and "pardon me." I don't think it was enough to impress the inspector. Do they send you back for not knowing English? Surely not!

The inspector wanted to know where Zalman was so they could tell him we had arrived and he needed to come get us. I tried to remember where Zalman lives, but I don't think anyone ever told me. If only Esther knew and wouldn't be too terrified to open her mouth!

That night they put us in a dormitory to sleep. After steerage, it was heaven! But how long would we stay here? Would they ever let us into America?

The bunks were in three tiers, like on the ship, but instead of hard wood, they were taut canvas covered with clean white sheets ~ and they didn't rock or pitch but stayed blessedly still!

I took the middle.

Esther took the bottom again.

After all this time and all this distance, we were still nowhere! Esther said she told the inspector that Zalman lives somewhere in Houston. That was all she could recall from the address on the letters he had sent. We'll just have to hope that's enough for them to find him.

The dining room is so clean and orderly ~ and they serve kosher food! Is all America like this? A sign on the wall said NO CHARGE FOR MEALS HERE in six different languages, including Yiddish.

November 9, 1901

This morning at breakfast we had a wonderful surprise ~ sitting at one of the tables eating porridge was Samuel!

He looked so astonished to see us, his spoon froze in midair. (Samuel has to be very surprised not to eat!) Esther was so excited she rushed up and hugged him. I had no idea she considered him a friend like I do.

as for me, I hugged him for so long, he pulled away, sputtering that he would starve if I wouldn't let him eat,

We all jabbered at once, excited to be together again.

the luxuries of Ellis Island

soft, sweet-smelling soap, not coarse like at home

snacks of milk and crackers

This is a "jare."

This is a "tabyl."

This is "zuppa."

This is a "glis."

I couldn't stop reaching out to touch his hand, his shoulder, to prove to myself he was really there. But Samuel was worried. He had to name a sponsor, since he's not an adult, but no one in America was waiting for him. So he named the only American he knew ~ Zalman ~ hoping Zalman would go along with it. Now we have to make sure that when ~ if ~ they find Zalman, he vouches for all three of us. I would say Samuel's my brother, but his last name is on his passport.

November 16, 1901

The boy's name is Giacomo.

He's teaching me English by pointing to things and saying the words.

I'm working hard to learn English while I'm here. There's a little Italian boy who was detained for having ringworm on his scalp. (His whole family stayed with him.) They had to shave his head, but he's been here a month, so some fuzz has grown back. And more than hair, he's grown a whole new language. If only I can do the same!

November 25, 1901

We've been here for weeks and I'm beginning to wonder if they'll ever find Zalman. This morning an inspector told me that if we're still without a sponsor by next Wednesday, we'll be sent back! Esther cried at the news. Samuel said he would jump into the water and swim to America. But really what can we do? How can I disappoint my family?

strange american foods

banana ~ do **not** eat the outside!

ice cream ~ it's <u>supposed</u> to be cold

corn flakes

It looks like chicken feed, but it's not.

turkey ~ a **big** chicken

chewing gum ~ don't swallow

November 29, 1901

Yesterday started out bitterly, but it ended sweetly. No, Zalman has still not been found, but it was a special American holiday called Thanksgiving. Like Jewish festivals, there was a real feast for dinner ~ strange foods I'd never eaten before. There are <u>many</u> new things I've tasted since we arrived, but last night was the best. I would be even more thankful if we were allowed to stay in America.

pumpkin pie

creamy whipped potatoes

November 30, 1901

Giacomo and his family left for New York today. How I wish we could go with them. Still no sign of Zalman. Could something have happened to him? Is there anyone else we can ask to meet us? What about Reb Jozef's daughter, Shayna?

December 1, 1901

Only two more days before we'll be deported. It's bad enough that Esther and I must go back ~ I feel terrible that Samuel is bound to our fate as well. Another boat trip? Another storm? My Papashka's broken heart? My broken promise? How can I face all that? We can't go back, we <u>can't</u>!

Samuel certainly hasn't given up. He helps out in the kitchen, hoping to prove so useful the cook will let him stay.

samuel says he'd be happy staying right here.

We spend our days outside as much as we can bear the cold. Through the fence we can see the unimaginably tall buildings of New York.

If only we were birds and could fly there!

December 2, 1901

Esther and I discussed it and we've decided that if the worst happens ~ if we're forced to return ~ then Samuel mustn't be left alone and friendless. He must come back with us to our shtetl. Esther's family has no sons, they'll welcome Samuel with open hearts.

December 3, 1901

Our last day on Ellis Island! But rather than another steamship, we boarded a ferry for New York! Finally, finally, finally, the immigration agents found Zalman. All this time they'd been looking in Houston, Texas, far, far away, when he was really on Houston Street in New York, just across the harbor!

Zalman has a kind, gentle face and he welcomed Esther shyly. He was happy to be Samuel's sponsor, especially when he heard all Samuel has done for us.

It all happened so quickly, after being here so long. The agent showed us out the door to the "Kissing Post." (It's called that because so many families are reunited there ~ my family, too, I pray.) I was so happy, I could have kissed Zalman, stranger though he is!

New York, up close

So many people live in these buildings packed close together.

Zalman took us to his tenement building. A home in America! Other people from our shtetl live in the same rooms. The old butcher and his family, Reb Jozef's Shayna, and now the three of us (Zalman, too, of course) are all here. So although it's a strange new home, it's also cozy and familiar.

December 4, 1901

Today was my first full day in America, and already so much has happened! Zalman took us to HIAS

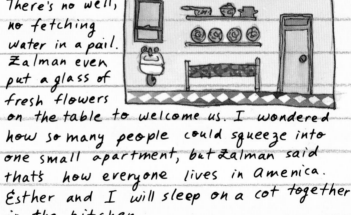

The apartment is small but clean. And it has the amazing luxury of water right from a tap! There's no well, no fetching water in a pail. Zalman even put a glass of fresh flowers on the table to welcome us. I wondered how so many people could squeeze into one small apartment, but Zalman said that's how everyone lives in America. Esther and I will sleep on a cot together in the kitchen.

(the Hebrew Immigration Aid Society), and the people there gave us clothes and, more importantly, jobs. Esther and I are working in a clothing factory and Samuel is at a canning factory. We start the day after tomorrow!

Zalman has a flush toilet down the hall from his apartment. He explained to us how to use it. Now I know why the toilets at Ellis Island were always clogged — you're not supposed to put trash in them!

Vendors sell everything from pots to shoes to bagels to books!

I chose <u>Tom Sawyer</u>. Esther picked <u>Huckleberry Finn</u>.

What funny names for books!

To celebrate we each bought one American book, so we can start to read. Zalman laughed and said we should choose books <u>after</u> we know English because how else can we know what we're buying? But I don't care — just having an American book makes me feel more American and like I'm learning already.

As wonderful as getting the jobs was, HIAS gave us one more thing — they enrolled us in night school to learn English. I will finally get to go to school! Papashka will be so proud! I <u>knew</u> America was a wonderful place — and not just because of coffee and doughnuts. Here they give away education — it costs nothing!

The lady at HIAS gave me a new pencil to start my studies with. What a delicious smell it has, the smell of learning!

December 5, 1901

I know tomorrow will be hard. It's our first day at the factory. Zalman has told us that conditions are terrible. But listening to him joke about his own job and all the things he's learned, I'm impatient to start mine, to make my own way in this new world.

Samuel started at the cannery yesterday. As usual he's already an expert at managing things, not a greenhorn like us.

He's already charmed the boss and talked him into allowing Samuel to take home a dented can or two.

And each day of hard work brings my family closer. That's all that matters.

Today Samuel and I made an amazing discovery. We were out

Esther has truly bloomed in America! Suddenly she's talkative, friendly even. Not to me but to Zalman! It's clear from her blushes that she likes him ~ and he likes her.

Now that she isn't pretending to be Rivka, she's changed her hair back.

walking, exploring this great city, when we came to a building that was so magnificent I was sure it was a palace. We stood there, gaping, and then I noticed that ordinary people were going in and out of it, people who looked like me and Samuel.

"Shall we try?" Samuel asked, the familiar glint in his eye. I was scared, but curious, too, so I nodded, and slowly we walked up the stairs.

Once we got to the top, before the grand doors, I was too timid to dare to actually go in. I was about to turn and leave, but Samuel grabbed my hand and pulled me in. (For once I was the one being forced through a door!) And there we were, in the most beautiful place I've ever seen.

There were long tables to read at. Each person had their own little lamp, their own private pool of light. It was truly magical!

The room was elegant, but what caught my eye were the books. There were books everywhere and people, ordinary people, sitting at the tables reading them.

A woman came up to us and I thought she would shoo us out, but she didn't. She spoke gently and gave us each a little card and pointed to all the books. They are for <u>us</u>, these books! We are allowed to read any book we want! That's my idea of paradise. That's my idea of America. And I promised myself I would read every single book.

Even though we can't read English yet, Samuel and I sat down and leafed through a book. Just staring at the words and turning the pages made me feel I was turning myself into a reader. Every few minutes, I would catch Samuel's eye, and we would giggle with excitement. We had found the gold that people had said paved America's streets, and we felt <u>very</u> rich!

I wrote to Papashka and Mama and told them all our wonderful news. It's hard to explain America, so much is different here. I copied out the letter so I can

I imagine them outside under the trees. Does it sound silly to miss trees? I can't help it — I do!

read it over and over again, imagining them reading it and thinking about me. Then they don't seem so far away after all.

December 5, 1901

Dear Papashka and Mama,

At last we are truly here, in America! And it is just as wonderful a place as everyone says. Not that there's gold in the streets, but I already have a job and my wages are $1.50 a week! By summer I'll be able to send for Isadore.

Best of all, I'M GOING TO SCHOOL! Do you believe it? In America everyone can go to school without even paying for it! I've already learned to speak a little English and I'm trying to read it, too. Imagine, now I know three alphabets! I've even bought my first American book, so now I have two books.

I wish I could show you all the marvels here. There is a beautiful building called a library where anyone can sit and read any book they like. It's more wonderful than any dream. But even with all these miracles, I think of you every moment. I will work as hard as I can so we can all be together again soon.

Your loving daughter, Hannahle

# GLOSSARY

**Cossacks** a group of armed frontiersmen who patrolled Russia's borders

**haroset** a sweet mixture of chopped apples, nuts, and wine served during the Passover seder

**heder** Hebrew school

**kiddush** the ritual blessing over the wine said before the Sabbath meal

**"nu"** an expression of impatience, meaning "So?" or "Well?"

**Papashka** an affectionate variation of "Papa"

**pogrom** an organized attack on a group of helpless people, such as Jews

**Reb** a respectful title, similar to "Mister"

**rebbe** rabbi or teacher

**seder** the ceremonial feast held on the Jewish holiday of Passover to commemorate the exodus from Egypt

**"sha"** a soothing expression to quiet or calm, like "shhh"

**Shabbat** the Jewish Sabbath, beginning at sundown Friday and lasting through Saturday evening

**sheyna** "pretty one"

**shtetl** a village

**tsar** the ruler of Russia before the 1917 revolution

*Hannah's Journal* is a work of fiction based on the lives of many immigrants, including the author's relatives, who entered the United States through Ellis Island. Although some of the experiences described in the book are drawn from real life, the characters are all creations of the author's imagination.

www.harcourt.com

First Silver Whistle paperback edition 2002
*Silver Whistle* is a trademark of Harcourt, Inc., registered in the United States of America and/or other jurisdictions.

Library of Congress Cataloging-in-Publication Data
Moss, Marissa.
Hannah's journal: the story of an immigrant girl/Marissa Moss.
p. cm.—(Young American Voices)
"Silver Whistle."
Includes glossary.
Summary: In the Russian shtetl where she and her family live, Hannah is given a diary for her tenth birthday, and in it she records the dramatic story of her journey to America.
[1. Emigration and immigration—Fiction. 2. Jews—Russia—Fiction. 3. Russia—Fiction. 4. Jews—United States—Fiction. 5. Diaries—Fiction.]
I. Title. II. Series.
PZ7.M8535Han 2000
[Fic]—dc21    99-35651
ISBN 0-15-202155-8
ISBN 0-15-216329-8 (pb)

A C E G H F D B
C E G H F D (pb)

The illustrations in this book were done in watercolor, gouache, and ink.
The text type was hand-lettered by Marissa Moss.
The display type was set in Opti Packard-C.
Manufactured by South China Printing Company, Ltd., China
Production supervision by Sandra Grebenar and Wendi Taylor
Designed by Lori McThomas Buley and Hannah

# Author's Note

During the peak years of immigration, between 1900 and 1920, more than fourteen million people entered the United States. They came mostly from Europe, but also from Asia, Africa, the Caribbean, and the Middle East. Most people born in America today can trace their family histories to the gates of Ellis Island.

Although <u>Hannah's Journal</u> is a work of fiction my own great-grandmother's journey to America provided much of the basis for Hannah's story. Like Hannah, she came with not much more than a Shabbat tablecloth and dreams of an education.

The character of Samuel is also based on a real person, my great-uncle Sam. Like Samuel, my great-uncle hid under the floorboards of his house during a Cossack raid and **traveled all** the way to America by himself at the age of ten. As a child I was riveted whenever he told me his story ~ it all sounded so dramatic and impossibly far away. But Sam's story was true, and like the character Samuel, he was detained on Ellis Island because of a simple confusion between a street's name and a city's.

Still, Hannah's journal is not just family history. Aspects of her story are drawn from the large body of immigrant literature and history. Journals like Hannah's lie in dusty attics or locked in grandparents' memories. They are all American stories, waiting to be told.

# Other exciting titles by Marissa Moss in the Young American Voices series:

### Rachel's Journal: The Story of a Pioneer Girl

Traveling by covered wagon, young Rachel and her family follow the Oregon Trail from Illinois all the way to California. The terrain is rough and the seven-month trip is filled with adventure. Rachel's own handwritten journal chronicles every detail as she and her family make their way to their new home in California.

### Emma's Journal: The Story of a Colonial Girl

The year is 1774, and the American Revolution for independence from the British is underway. Emma wants desperately to help the American struggle for freedom. When Papa gives her a secret code the militia uses, Emma finally gets her chance to change the course of history.

### Rose's Journal: The Story of a Girl in the Great Depression

On January 1, 1935, Rose Samuels bids good riddance to a dry, desolate year and begins a new one. The severe drought has left the fields too dry for crops. Times are tough all over, but armed with hope, love, and determination, Rose and her family manage to turn the year around. *Rose's Journal* chronicles the heroic progress of an ordinary family living in the Dust Bowl.

**Marissa Moss** is best known for her handwritten and illustrated journals, including those in the Young American Voices series. She also writes and illustrates the wildly popular *Amelia's Notebook* series, including *Amelia's Notebook*, *Amelia Writes Again*, *Amelia Hits the Road*, and *Amelia Takes Command*. Ms. Moss lives in Berkeley, California.